Year Two: Love and Revenge

Chapter One: A Ship in the Night

Written By: Jeremy Whitley

Art By: Xenia Pamfil

Lettered By: Justin Birch

Edited By: Nicole D'Andria

PRINCELESS: RAVEN THE PIRATE PRINCESS: YEAR TWO #1, November 2017. Copyright Jeremy Whitley,2016. Published by Actio

Katie? Have you guys seen Katie?
Nope.
Haven't seen her.
Is she lost? Oh no!
Gone, have you seen Katie?
On.
Did that sound like I said no? You know, since I'm upside down?
Gone, it's time to eat. Go join everybody else.
On! On on on on on!
There you are.
Katie... what are you doing?

Trish, I think I messed this up somewhere.
That depends. Were you trying to cook something for the party or burn the ship down?
Because if it's the second one...
But I'm a really good coo I wanted to sho everybody.
Well, the party is starting, so whatever you ended up with will have to do.
It's starting? Rats! This is gonna be terrible.
Hold this.
Katie, I'm sure you're a great cook, but being at sea is about working with what you have.
I know...
And setting up the sandbox in a room with proper ventilation.
That explains why I nearly passed out.
Yeah, let's try not to die in a fire on the open sea.

I think we're the last ones. Verity and Helena are on deck, but everybody made something.
I hope mine isn't the worst.
Sunshine? Where are you going? Aren't you going to eat?
Yeah, I'm not hungry. I'm feeling nauseous all of a sudden.
Should we go after her?
Let her be. I'm sure she'll come back eventually.
Katie and Trish!

My father was a swordfighter, I guess it sort of runs in the family.
My brother is not so much for fighting. He's more of an engineer, like me.
So what if we ranked every dish from best to worst? Would you want to be a judge?
I can't imagine anything I'd want to do less. In fact-

See, you carry all your stress right here in your shoulders.
I... umm... humma.
Ooh, this looks promising.
You and I have different definitions for that word.

--If you want to keep your ears intact, I'd recommend skipping the seat next to Zoe.
Dezzy, where are you going?
Cause trouble. Save lives.
This was supposed to be a whole crew thing. If you leave-
I would stop and describe to you how little I care, but I just don care enough to do that.
Captain. Reporting with... well, I'm not sure what to call it. I'm worried it's terrible.
I'm sure it's great, Katie. I know you've been working on it all day. Right, Ray?
Huh?
Now Raven, if you can't function as a human being while I rub your shoulders, I'm going to have to stop.
Huh? What? What happened? Why stop?
Katie was telling you about the food she brought. I stopped so you could talk to her.
Katie... that's twice now.

Raven!
Hah! I'm kidding! I'm sure it's great Katie. You're the greatest.
Thanks. Don't let me break this up. Ximena, I know for me it's my neck. Have you tried running your hand up from the base of her skull through her hair?
Oooh! That sounds like fun. You game?
Okay.
BANG!
Unf!
I think she likes it, Katie.
Raven, you still with us?
Whoa.
Gah!
Leave me here. Go on without me.

No, I'm as opposite as it gets. No siblings. No parents. I was sort of adopted by a sea captain who taught me how to take care of myself.
See, now that sounds like the life to me. Siblings are the worst.
You say that, but until this group I never really had a friend who wasn't forty something.
See, having siblings is a poor solution to wanting friends. I moved out because there was no room for me.
Hey, you two?
You see a pouty six-foot-tall ball of emotion come through here?
She's up in the crow's nest. What do you want with her?
Yeah, I heard what happened last time you picked a fight with Sunshine.
My fault, I know it sounded like I wanted you two to ramble on pointlessly.
And now there's climbing. This had better be worth it.

=sniff=
I hope you're not into any freaky stuff up here, elf girl.
That was a lie. I kinda hoped you were.
Oh good, and I thought this day couldn't get worse.
See, that's the junk I've had enough of. Where's the annoyingly perky half-breed that I've grown to love slash hate?
Don't call me that.
I come in peace. Mostly.
Listen, height matters and we can't let the short girls win.
What?
I know we've had our differences, but I'm Team Ravenshine all the way.
I know you want to make me miserable but–
What I want is for you to get the girl. Now are you with me or are you just gonna keep moping?
I'm listening.

Okay, hard questions, and be honest. You're totally into Raven, right?
I mean–

Elf Girl! I've seen how you look at her. She was leaning over the edge pulling up the anchor the other day and you nearly bit your lip off.
Okay, yeah.
Say it.

I am WAY into my captain. Like, I've already named the two dogs we'll have together. I planned our trip to the desert so she can see–
Okay, gah, spare me the gooshy details.

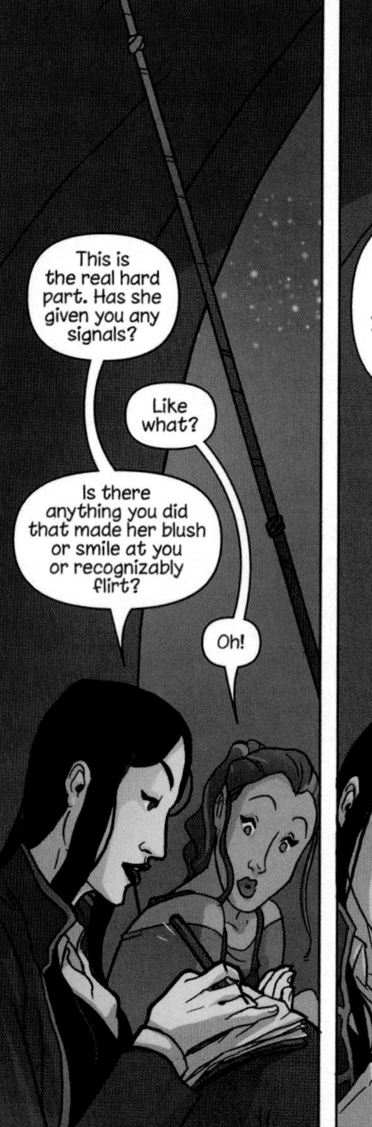
This is the real hard part. Has she given you any signals?
Like what?
Is there anything you did that made her blush or smile at you or recognizably flirt?
Oh!

Dancing! When I danced at Cookie's she told I was beautiful. She couldn't take her eyes off me.
Oh, that we can work with. Did you bring any short dresses you can dance in? Ximena's whatever, but you're miles ahead in the legs department
Are you kidding? I've one that more leg than Ximena's got.

"And I look amazing in it."
Listen up ladies! Somebody told me we were having a party, is that right?
YEAH!!!
I just... I like dancing, okay?
Everybody have a seat and keep your eyes up here as we present tonight's entertainment.
Excuse me, I'm gonna slide in here.
Sunshine, show them what you've got.
Let's do this.

Come dance with me.
I don't really know how.
Don't worry, I'll go easy on you.
What should I do? How do I-
Stop asking questions and just have fun.
I'll try and keep up.
Just think of it like fighting, but wit less punching and more of this-

Okay, don't let them have all the fun. Grab a partner and head to the floor!
Or grab two partners! Or no partners!
Just do you!
And I know it's going to be hard, but try not to fall in love with me.
I'll do my best.
What do you say X, can you dance?
Try to stop me.

"Dance?"
"Yes."
You goin' up there?
Huh? Oh no, nobody wants that.
It'll be fun.
Not for me, but don't let me stop you.
Trish! I need somebody who's willing to make my dancing look less dumb by pretending they're deliberate.
Ha. Okay, count me in.

I don't do dancing. Not your thing either?
I'm ready for the next mission. Give me some brawling or sword fighting, right?
Nah.
Yeah, I guess.
Dezzy, can I talk to you?
I'm a little busy at the moment.
I see what you're doing and you need to stay out of it.
Amirah, I have no idea what you're talking about.
You're a troublemaker, Desideria. It's going to catch up with you.
Lighten up Amirah, enjoy yourself.
Hmph!
That's what Ximena and I are doing, right babe?
You should dance, Amirah! You'll feel better.

Ya said ya don't dance, but you've got me sweating up a storm. You want to go somewhere cooler?
Lead the way.

Uh-oh! Get 'em Zoe.
You got this, Trish!
GO! GO! GO! GO!
Oh goddess, are they not the cutest?
They are.
I don't know, destiny doesn't make sense to me. I think we have to fight to make a good future.
See, I just think I'm the one at the wheel.
I'm not saying don't fight. But I believe we're being steered to where we're supposed to be.
I see what you did there.

That was so
much fun! And you
didn't think you
could dance!
You're
the one with
all the skill. I
just followed
along.
Thank you
for pulling me in.
I never would have
danced without you.
You were right
about it being like
fighting.
Well, I'm
glad you didn't
punch me. I got
enough of that
on our first
date.
Our
first-
Ha ha!
Are you calling
you robbing me,
breaking my nose,
and knocking me
unconscious our
first date?
The way
I remember it,
I kissed you and we
ended up rolling
around behind a bar
together.
Either
way, sparks
flew from the
first time
we met.
I'll agree
to that.
You
know...
...there's
something I've
been wondering
since that
day.
What's
that?
Did I make
it up? Was it as
amazing as I remember
it being? If I did it
again, would it be
as good?
What
EXACTLY are
you talking
about?
Let
me show
you.

BOOM!!

Even better the second time.
Wow.
I... that was amazing. Where did you learn to kiss like that?
Just now, I think. It was amazing, right?
My eyes were closed, but I could have sworn there was an explosion.
I felt the same thing. Like fireworks.
But... what about–
Don't say it. Let me hold on to the moment before something ruins it.
INCOMING!
What?
Incoming?

SPLECK!
CRACK
RAVEN!
I CAN'T SWIM!
Sunshine!
SPLASH

Captain, hostile approaching starboard. What do we do?
Muster the crew. Katie's in charge until I get back.
Back?
Sunshine? Sunshine?! Where are you?

SUNSHINE!
SUN-
CRACK!

Unused Cover for Raven: The Pirate Princess Volume One

Raven sketches by Xenia

Pages 4-5 Progression

Pages 4-5:

Panel 1: Two page spread. This is the galley. It is lit by several lamps throughout the room. The only crew members missing from this shot should be Verity, Helena, and Sunshine (who are up on deck).

The cause of Sunshine's frustrations sits at the end of the table. Raven is sitting at the end of the table. Ximena is standing behind Raven, rubbing her shoulders. Raven is putty in her hands. Raven is starry eyed and looking as if she is experiencing profound pleasure and relaxation.

Elsewhere at the table, Cid is teaching Jayla sign language.

Pirate, Melody, and Ophelia are looking through a number of prepared foods that dot the table. Some of them look downright delicious, some look pretty awful. They're all things that (with a little latitude) they should be able to make on the ship with only a couple of days at sea. Pirate and Ophelia have some food on their plates but Melody has already stacked hers high.

Quinn is talking to Amirah. Zoe is chatting a bored Desideria's ear off. Gone is in the background, not doing much as usual.

XIMENA
See, you carry all your stress right here in your shoulders.

RAVEN
I…umm…humma.

PIRATE
Ooh, this looks promising.

OPHELIA
You and I have different definitions for that word.

QUINN
My father was a swordfighter, I guess it sort of runs in the family.

AMIRAH
My brother is not so much for fighting. He's more of an engineer, like me.

ZOE
So what if we ranked every dish from best to worst? Would you want to be a judge?

DESIDERIA
I can't imagine anything I'd want to do less. In fact--

Page 11 Progression

Page 11:

Panel 1: Desideria walks into the galley, now wearing dancing clothes. She is setting up a Victrola.

SUNSHINE (CAPTION)
…And I look amazing in it.

DESIDERIA
Listen up ladies! Somebody told me we were having a party, is that right?

MELODY
YEAH!!!

Panel 2: Melody looks around shyly as the other girls regard her in confusion.

MELODY
I just…I like dancing, okay?

Panel 3: Desideria moves Ximena from behind Raven to a seated position next to Raven.

DESIDERIA
Everybody have a seat and keep your eyes up here as we present tonight's entertainment.

Panel 4: Desideria seats herself between Raven and Ximena.

DESIDERIA
Excuse me, I'm gonna slide in here.

DESIDERIA
Sunshine, show them what you've got.

Panel 5: Sunshine peeks her head around the corner, excited.

SUNSHINE
Let's do this.

Pages 12-13 Progression

Pages 12-13:

Panel this however you would like. Have fun with it. If you want to give Sunshine a new dress, I'm fine with that. Something attractive and leggy, but that makes sense for dancing. You know. She should really own these two pages. If you want to throw in a reaction shot from Raven, that's fine. It should end with her spinning up next to Raven and stopping (potentially with her foot on Raven's chair/bench.)

Page 24 Progression

Page 24:

Panel 1: Raven dives again. There are pieces of flotsam and jetsam but nothing else is visible.

Panel 2: Raven is floating underwater, looking around. Everything is darkness.

Panel 3: Raven goes back to the surface.

Panel 4: Raven looks around. We can see the other ship closing in the distance.

RAVEN
SUNSHINE! SUN—

Panel 5: A falling piece of the ship hits Raven in the head.

SFX
Crack!

Panel 6: Darkness.

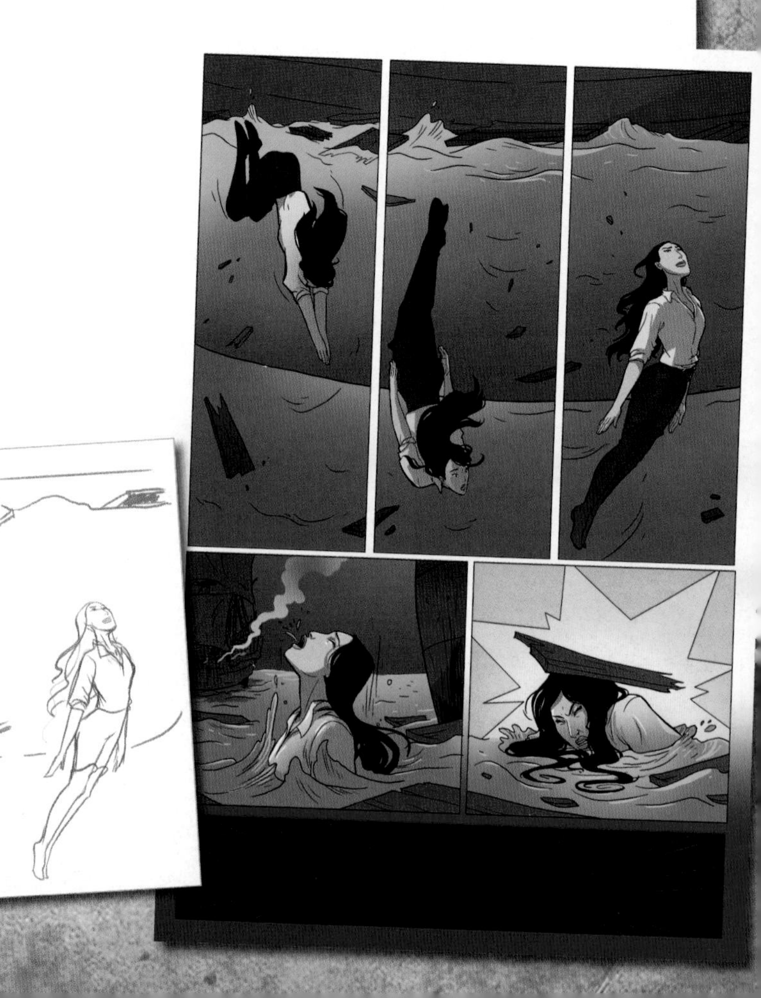

Year Two: Love and Revenge

Chapter Two: Overboard

Written By: Jeremy Whitley

Art By: Xenia Pamfil

Lettered By: Justin Birch

Edited By: Nicole D'Andria

Variant Cover By: Sorah Suhng and Kate Flash

PRINCELESS: RAVEN THE PIRATE PRINCESS: YEAR TWO #2, December 2017. Copyright Jeremy Whitley,2016. Published by Actio
Lab Entertainment. All rights reserved. All characters are fictional. Any likeness to anyone living or dead is purely coincidental. No p
of this publication may be reproduced or transmitted without permission, except for review purposes. Printed in Canada. First Printi

So, Dezzy, why me?
Huh?
Why'd you pick me to dance with? You've barely said a word to me before.
Oh, that?
I was just helping Sunshine.
Sunshine?
You know, getting you out of the way so she could have a shot with Raven.
What are you- where are they?
Oh, they went up to the deck a minute ago. You're probably-
-too late!
BOOM!

Oh my god!
Verity, what is it?!
Where's Raven?
The railing broke and Sunshine fell!
The Captain dove in after her, but I think she's hurt. I haven't seen her come up!
NO! This is terrible!
Katie, give me your dagger.
Listen to me, Katie. You're in charg here and thes girls look to you.
Wait.
I don't know what to do.
This ship is about to be boarded. You have to repel them.
You can do that. I know you can.
What are you doing?
Well, I don't fight, s I'm gonna try a go rescue my my Raven.

Lower the lifeboat so I can get out.
Make her proud, because I'm bringing her back.
I will.

SPLASH!

Where'd you go, Raven?

Okay Kling, you can do this. They're depending on you.
Katie? What do we do?
We defend this ship.
Everybody listen up!
The captain is pulling Sunshine out of the drink, so I'm in charge here.
I don't know who these jerks are, but they just attacked us without warning and they're about to try and board this ship.
We're not gonna let that happen!
We came here to test our mettle.
We came here because we're sick of being treated as lesser than. We're sick of being disregarded.
This ship is our chance for a new life! They don't get to take that!

WE ARE WOMEN!
WE ARE MIGHTY!
NOW MAKE THEM SORRY THEY EVER THOUGHT THEY COULD STOP US!

Get 'em, Free Women!

You don't know how long I've been waiting for this!
I'll run ye through, wench!
Don't call me-
-WENCH!
NEXT!

En garde.
Look at you! You have no idea how to use a sword.
Har! I'm gonna cut you to ribbons!
Wouldn't count on it.
SWIP
SWIP!
You're fast!
♫♪♫
And you're slow.

Come on! It's getting crowded in here, Raven!
There!

Come on, Ray. I've got you.
Ergh!
This is not how I pictured this night going.
No breathing. Okay, I can do this.

One, two, three, four, five, six, seven.
There you go. On your side.
cough cough
cough cough
I've got you. I've got you.
Sunshine–
Sunshine is still out there.

HTSSSSSEEEEE

What are you two whelps doing in here?
What kind of nonsense is–
Argh! I'm stuck.

Where does
e go to get this
any disposable
sleazeballs?
They've gotta have some kind of outlet store, right?
Buy your henchmen by the dozen. Who's in charge here, anyway?
I'd guess him.
Don't take this lying down you billowing bilgewater foul-smelling swine!
They're just a bunch of useless girls. They should be no match for the crew of Melancholy Johnny!
What are the
odds he knows the
orrect meaning of
melancholy?
Switch?
Less likely than a parrot, but more likely than a carp?
Switch!
Aargh!
Rarr!

This is not going how I'd hoped.
Not as strong as you thought, eh? Weak women have no business in battle.
Try me on for size, you mangy cur!
Argh!
There you go, Pirate!
How's this for a weak woman?
Work the body! Work the body!
POW!
That was satisfying.
Hey, where'd Melody get off to?

Sunshine?! Sunshine, where are you?!
What is-
A piece of her dress? Oh goddess!

Come here, little girl! You're gonna learn why you don't pick a fight with Melancholy Johnny!
But I didn't-
Excuses already? I figured at least have to h you before thos started.
But I didn't try to fight you! You're much-
Aaaah!
Not ready to be one of the men now, are you?
Not a mistake you'll live to repeat.
Dana Johnathan Christie!
What cow dares t call me that name?

I do! Remember me?
If I had seen that ugly mug before, I must have worked hard to forget it.
Don't lie to me, Dana–
It is. I know because I know you.
Don't call me that! It's not my name!
Wait a minute! You're the fat girl who wanted to be a pirate! Cassie, was it?
Wrong. I'm the fat girl who's twice the pirate you ever were.
Since when? I wouldn't let you join my crew, remember?
I remember that I passed every physical test you put in front of me and then you humiliated me.
Hardly! You didn't pass the weight test! You were too heavy to be on my ship.
Well, I'm a pirate now.
Oh, is that what you call this group of sea cows? Even this door-mouse here?
Ooowww!
TWIST

Tell you what, chubs. Let's you and me settle this mano a... whatever you are.
Fine by me. Let the girl go.
Do I have to explain everything to you? We shake hands to seal the deal. Only then am I going to let this creature live.
Fine.
Let's shake hands and you let her go.
Well, look at that. You can teach a dog to shake hands. I never believed that was a real thing.
Give me just a second here...

Ha!
Awww!
Are you okay? This looks bad.
Katie!
Shaking hands is for gentlemen, Cassie! Just because you're bad at being a woman doesn't make you a man.
Now, back to me killing you one on one.
Hold still. Let me try nd stop the bleeding.
You maniac! She's bleeding all over the place! Besides, what's gonna stop us all from teaming up on you?
Nothing, I suppose.
Owww!
Well, except that. But pirate ships lose crew members, right? It happens.

You're garbage, Johnny! You deserve to rot in the depths! I'll send you there myself!
Wait, Trish.
Hold this, Amirah.
You shouldn't be doing this. You-
Don't worry. Me and Dana go back a long way, don't we?
Well Dana-
STOP CALLING ME THAT!
Make me.

Blah!
Come on. She's gotta be around here somewhere, right? Come on Ximena, you can–
That's her in the boat!
That's the Black Arrow!
Magpie'll ay a huge eward for her!
No!
There's another one! Shoot her before she gets in there!
PLANK!
PLINK!
PLANK!

Come on! Anybody up there?! Help us!
Errrgh!
Gah!
Please, somebody. I can't let her die. I can't. I... I lo-
Thank you.

Character sketches
by Xenia
XENIA

Character sketches
by Xenia
XENIA

Character sketches
by Xenia

Pages 11 & 12 Progression

Page 11:

Panel 1: Ximena holds Raven's nose and breaths directly into her mouth.

Panel 2: Ximena puts her hands together on Raven's sternum and begins compressions.

XIMENA
One, two, three, four, five, six, seven.

Panel 3: Raven starts coughing up water.

RAVEN
Cough cough.

XIMENA
There you go. On your side.

Panel 4: Ximena rolls Raven over, still sitting on her.

RAVEN
Cough cough.

Panel 5: Ximena collapses on top of Raven.

XIMENA
I've got you. I've got you.

RAVEN
Sunshine—

Panel 6: Ximena bites her lip, trying to decide what to do.

RAVEN
Sunshine is still out there.

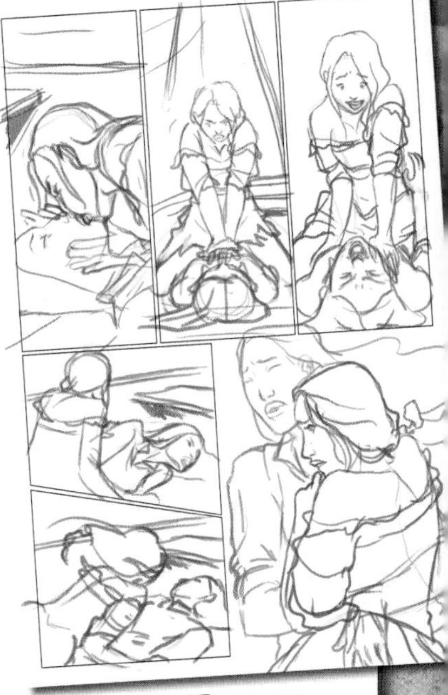

Page 11 Thumbnail

Page 12:

Panel 1: Jayla and Cid are in the hold of the ship, packing backpacks full of supplies.

Panel 2: Jayla pulls a cannon away from a port, leaving an opening. Cid is tying the end of a rope to the cannon.

Panel 3: Cid aims a crossbow out the window, the arrow is attached to a rope.

Panel 4: The arrow with the rope fires into the opposite port.

Panel 5: Cid and Jayla zip across the rope with the pully devices they made in issue 7.

Page 12 Thumbnail

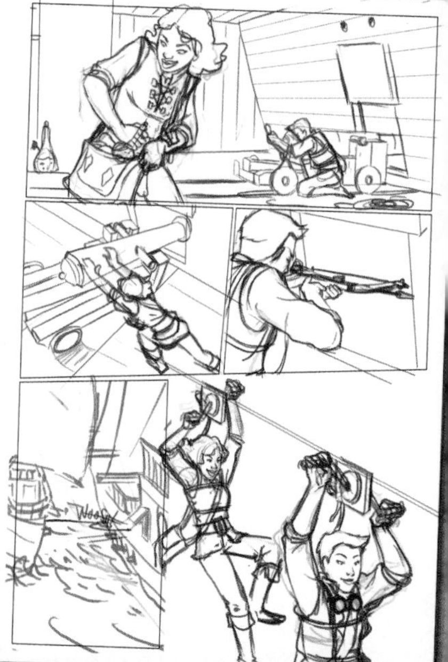

Page 11 Progression
Page 11 Inks
Page 11 Colors

Page 12 Progression
Page 12
Inks
Page 12 Colors

Year Two:
Love and Revenge

Chapter Three:
The Ballad of Katie Kling

Written By: Jeremy Whitley

Art By: Xenia Pamfil

Lettered By: Justin Birch

Edited By: Nicole D'Andria

Variant Cover By: Sorah Suhng and Kate Flash

PRINCELESS: RAVEN THE PIRATE PRINCESS: YEAR TWO #3, December 2017. Copyright Jeremy Whitley,2016. Published by Actic
Lab Entertainment. All rights reserved. All characters are fictional. Any likeness to anyone living or dead is purely coincidental. No p
of this publication may be reproduced or transmitted without permission, except for review purposes. Printed in Canada. First Print

Come on, girls! Easy now.
Gone, how did you even know they were there? You couldn't have heard them.
Put it down gently.
Do you think they're alright?
I don't know, Zoe.
Ximena's shot. It's not fatal, but–
Owwww...
–it looks painful.
We'll have to fix that.
Raven's still breathing.

You'll have to get through us.

You heard her boys. Get the Black Arrow.

You're pathetic, Dana.
My name is Melancholy Johnny!
No, it's not.
When I'm done with you, I'll cut it into your ugly face so you remember next time.
Dana, you've got iss-
Arrrgh!
Yeah, dummy, I stabbed you under your sword arm.
You can't fight without pulling on it.
Don't worry, it won't hurt for long.

Ophelia, Pirate– we're going to get Melody.
Lead the way.
Say goodnight, girly!
No!
Come on Mel, let's get you safe.
I'm not sure any of us are safe here.
I think Helena might be.
You would attack an injured woman?
She had it coming.
And you've got this coming.

Argh!
How's it feel?
That little wench is a maniac!
More of you? Good.
CRACK!
POW!
A little wench, am I? Come here and take your punishment.

Where is she?
Sunshine has to be down there. Where?
Desideria! I could use some help here!
Huh?
I'm about to die here! This is going poorly!
It's my fault. I killed her.
Dezzy!

CRACK!
Was this guy bothering you?
You dropped this.
Catch!

There you go. Ready to rock some faces?
I think I might be too low level for this fight.
Ha!

Then stick with me, we'll get you some XP.
I'll watch your six.

Watch it as close as you like, just make sure you remember to fight too.

CLANG
Gah!
Oh, this is rich. You're going to try and fight me with your off hand now?
Give it up, girl. Your crew shouldn't have to watch me behead you right here. Think about these poor girls.
I am.
Give up now and I'll let most of them go.
No you won't.

Otherwise they'll end up as serving wenches for Crow. And Crow does not treat his wenches kindly.
No one on this crew is going to serve you or–
Hurts, doesn't it?
Aaaah!
Just give in. Just one quick cut and it's all over.
HA HA HA HA.
What's so funny?
You gave up your advantage.
See, people think ords are a close range apon, but they're not.
You ed room swing them.
Once you get this close-
-you're easily disarmed!

You can't stab me from this close.
But guess what?
Get off–
HEADBUTT!
You cow! How dare you strike my face!
Easy.
LIKE THIS!
BASH!

Oh, Dana. It's not looking so good for you anymore, is it?
I'm not the one bleeding everywhere!
I can fix that. Get back up.
Come on Dana, get back up so I can knock you back down.
Hold your horses.

Not this time, chump.
Psst, Dana! This is going to hurt.

KER-SLAM!
That's a tough one. Rough on the back.
You still with us there, Dana?
Bubububu...
The rest of you got two options. You can stay here and end up like him.
Or you get this trash off my deck and back over to-

-Where's your ship?
Whoa!
Oh.
ZRRRRRRP!

I guess you'll be piling onto the lifeboats. Unless anyone wants to keep fighting?
No? Good.
Get those boats cast off. Leave them with a map if you can.
Aye, captain.
Is there anyone missing?
Well... Sunshine. Ximena never–
I know.
And... I don't see Helena.
Find her, see if she needs help.
Aye, captain.
Katie? Are you... carrying me?
Aye, captain. Do you want me to put you down?
No. This is really comfy. Nobody's ever carried me before.

Helena? Are you back here?
Oh no.
Helena! Are you okay? Oh, you've got blood on your hands.
It's not mine. It's...I did something terrible.

What's in-
Oh no. What happ-
He was going to kill Melody. He was evil. I was just going to-
Captain, we're still missing a man.
As are we, but feel free to search for him before you leave.
We have to get rid of this.
But how could I do this? They should know.

It doesn't do them any good to know.
But the other girls. If they know what I did...
They're not going to find out, Helena. Now help me.
Helena, he was a bad man. They were all bad men. He would have done the same to you.
Not like that. I lost control. I don't know what–
It doesn't matter. Get up and help me deal with this.
We'll figure it out, okay?
Okay.

Hold tight, lowering the boat.
SPLASH

What is this? Some kind of-
-joke?

Page 8 Progression

Page 8:

Panel 1: Quinn comes out of nowhere to dropkick the pirate facing Zoe.

SFX
Crack!

Panel 2: Quinn holds her sword and the pirate's sword, one in each hand as she stands. The pirate is out cold.

QUINN
Was this guy bothering you?

Panel 3: Quinn hooks her foot in the handle of Zoe's sword on the deck.

QUINN
You dropped this.

Panel 4: Quinn effortlessly kicks the sword up to Zoe's hands.

QUINN
Catch!

Panel 5: Zoe fumbles the sword.

Panel 6: Zoe further fumbles the sword.

Panel 7: Zoe finally get ahold of the sword before it falls.

Page 8 Inks

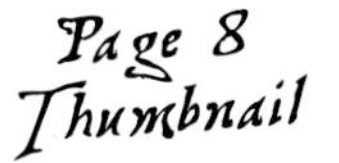

Page 8 Progression

Page 8 Colors

Page 12 Progression

Page 12:

Panel 1: Katie puts her arm over Johnny's arm, locking his arm in her armpit.

KATIE
You can't stab me from this close.

MELANCHOLY JOHNNY
Get off—

KATIE
But guess what?

Panel 2: Katie head-butts Johnny in the face, hard. Johnny loses his sword.

SFX
HEADBUTT!

Panel 3: Johnny stumbles, but his arm is caught under Katie's.

MELANCHOLY JOHNNY
You cow! How dare you strike my face!

KATIE
Easy.

Panel 4: Katie punches him in the face again. This time she allows him to stumble back away from her.

SFX
Bash!

Page 12 Inks

Page 12 Thumbnail

Page 12 Progression

Page 12 Colors

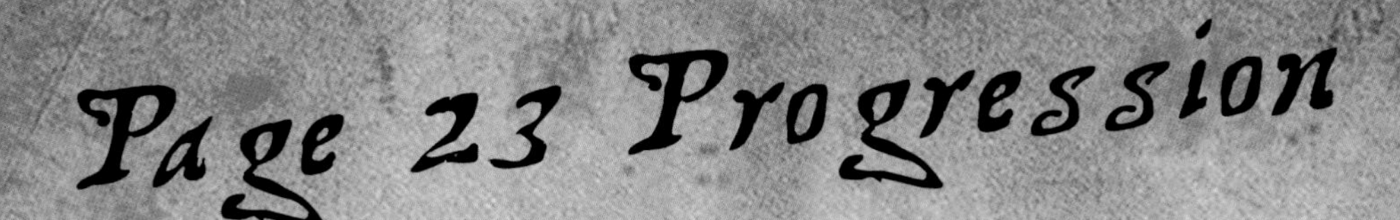

Page 23:

Panel 1: The pirates are on the lifeboat. Verity stands at the control, lowering it. The sun is starting to rise.

VERITY
Hold tight, lowering the boat.

Panel 2: The boat splashes into the water.

Panel 3: The boat rows to meet another boat.

Panel 4: Our ship leaves the lifeboats alone on the sea.

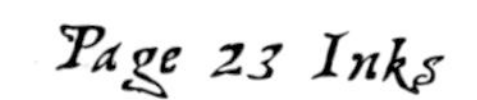

Page 23 Progression

Page 23 Colors

Year Two: Love and Revenge

Chapter Four: Stitches

Written By: Jeremy Whitley

Art (pages 1-21): Xenia Pamfil

Art (pages 22-24): Christine Hipp

Colors By: Xenia Pamfil

Lettered By: Justin Birch

Edited By: Nicole D'Andria

Main Cover By Xenia Pamfil

Variant Cover By: Sorah Suhng and Kate Flash

Bryan Seaton: Publisher/ CEO - Shawn Gabborin: Editor In Chief - Jason Martin: Publisher-Danger Zone
Nicole D'Andria: Marketing Director/Editor - Danielle Davison: Executive Administrator
Chad Cicconi: Deck Swabber - Shawn Pryor: President of Creator Relations

And... why am I holding your kindergarten craft project?
It's a sun, Quinn. A sun.
Okay, Desideria, why when I'm looking for herbs am I now holding your kindergarten craft project sun?
It's not mine. The girl gave it to me.
What l and why e you not swering my uestion?
Verity?
Jayla?
You know, the black one.
The weird black one.
No! Poofy hair. Kinda quiet. Creepy even.
OH MY GOD DEZZY!

Half the crew is injured. Stabbed, drowned, shot, and otherwise mangled. I came in here with Zoe to get some herbs and not only have you wasted my time–
-you've distracted me from helping people, proving once again how much you care about no one but yourself. You know what, I have one thing to say to–
Got it!
Time to help people rather than adding to the yelling.
BUT I LIKE YELLING!
MAYBE IF YOU WEREN'T SO BUSY STIRRING YOUR STUPID DRAMA, SUNSHINE WOULD STILL BE ALIVE.

That was a bit harsh, don't cha think?
Come on now. First all the drama with Sunshine, then freezing in the fight and-
DUCK!
Look ıt you! Saving / life again. You t can't stop now hat you've had a taste of it.
Don't tempt me. I get chaffed when people start expecting things of me.
Noted.
eaking of ich, she's e reason I d to save ur life in he first place.
Not that Sunshine was gone, but that it was her fault. Now she's making crafts?
She froze! She was traumatized.
She's gotta wake up eventually.
Just go easy on her. People deal with grief in different ways.
What's this on my shoulder?
A sign of my affection.
Take it away. Affection is gross and I don't want it. Clear?
As a bell.

Listen, Pirate and I barely even touched anybody.
I kicked one guy and then I felt my tights rip in a place they shouldn't be ripping.
He he.
See, there's the laugh. You're gonna be okay, Mel.
It just makes me so angry to lose to such a jerk.
Being a jerk doesn't make him a bad sword fighter.
I know.
I just... I always thought it would be like in a story where the guy is horrible and so I get a burst of strength.
Melody uses "Indignant Rage".
Melody is not plus five versus jerks and misogynists.
It's not very effective.
Awww... Melkins! Give me a hug.

We got the stuff. Well, mostly Zoe got the stuff and I–
Finally, someone useful!
I'm useful! You're just unreasonable!
ying to keep from bleeding death is not nreasonable!
he's trying hem me like a ir of pants!
THEY'RE CALLED STITCHES, KATHERINE!
You called her Katherine.
Woah.
Nobody ever calls me Katherine.
It won't matter what I call you if you're dead, will it?
Find Trish. Trish is the only one she'll listen to.
Aye aye.
Amirah, where'd you learn to do all this anyway?
It is a long story and not for today. Now bring me what I asked for.

By all means, this is your skill set.
What is?
Snooping, prying, finding people.
I...
You know what, I choose to take that as a compliment.
Hey, you are forever bothering me. I notice these things.
Hey, to be fair, I mostly bother you with things I know you're into.
And what am I into?
Punching, kicking, competing, making fun of things wi-
Zo!

Clumsy! That thing woulda cut you in half!
Mph mph mph!
I uh...ummm... phew...that is to say...
Yes?
Well, thank you, obviously... and...
And?
You called me Zo. Is that like a pet name? I've never had a pet name.
Maybe pet name is not the word I'm looking for.
I mean, pet names are for people you're in love with or something, right? And you don't do human affection.
I'll say.
Shut up, Zoe!
Aww...I liked Zo! Can I have Zo back?
SHUT UP, ZOE!
Do you know that your entire head and chest turns red when you blush? It must be the pale skin.

Drop it, Zoe. You know how much I like punching things.
But you love me, remember? You wouldn't punch me.
THUMP!
Ow!
I stand corrected.
Yes.
Can we find Trish now?
Thank you.

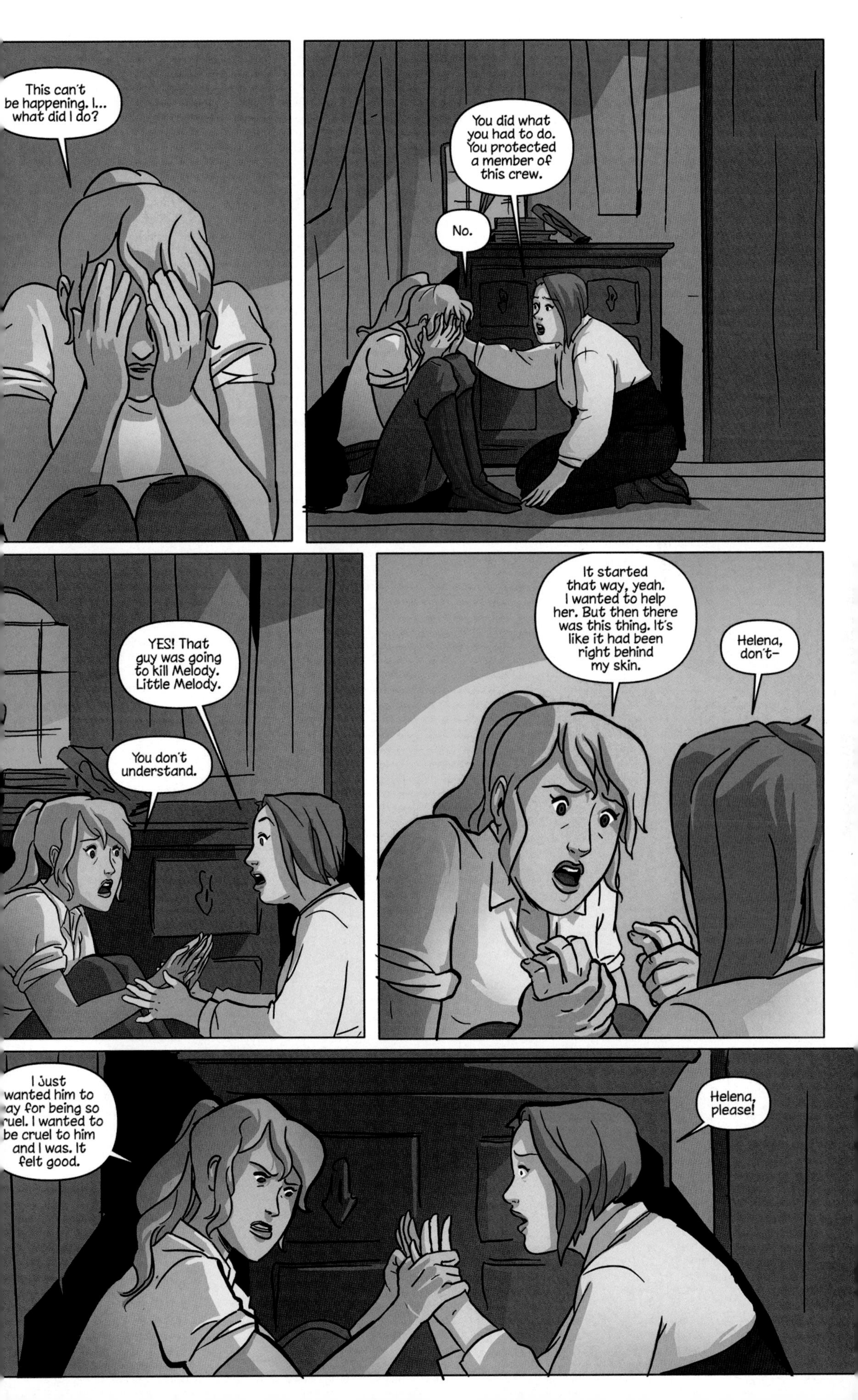
This can't be happening. I... what did I do?
You did what you had to do. You protected a member of this crew.
No.
YES! That guy was going to kill Melody. Little Melody.
You don't understand.
It started that way, yeah. I wanted to help her. But then there was this thing. It's like it had been right behind my skin.
Helena, don't–
I just wanted him to ay for being so ruel. I wanted to be cruel to him and I was. It felt good.
Helena, please!

Helena, you're hurting me.
Oh no, Trish! I didn't mean to. Are you okay?
I'm fine. I just-
Trish! Are you in here?!
Yes, hi, I'm here.
Yeah, hey.
Oh! Hi, Helena! I didn't know you were here too.
Hey... are you guys okay?
Yeah. We're fine. Helena just needed to talk priv-
Right, whatever, we're here to get you. Katie needs you.

Katie? I thought Amirah was working on her.
She won't let Amirah stitch her up. Amirah said you could convince her.
Errr.
So...are we all just going to stand around looking at each other meaningfully or–
I...
Are you gonna–
Are you sure?
I know. Go.
I'm okay.
Uh huh.
I'm not convinced.
Please go. I'm okay.

I hear the toughest woman on the seven seas is scared of needles?
Hey!
I am not "scared" of needles, okay. I am not ready to have someone sew me up like a torn sock though.
You big baby. If she doesn't sew it up it's going to get infected or worse.
There's got to be a better way.
Well, look at that.
Just keep holding still, you're doing a great job.
We're lucky to have you here, Amirah. If it weren't for you–
FINE!
I GET IT! Ximena is literally half my size and doesn't even fight. I'll let her stitch me up.
Thata girl!
But you gotta stay with me!

You know, X, for
meone that doesn't
fight you sure took
your share of the
punishment.
Right? Does
t look cool at
east? Tell me
it looks cool.
Maybe you'll get a scar and then you can tell stories about how you got it.
Kids, this is the scar from the time your mom dove off a moving boat to rescue your...
Oh my god, that's so great! I'm gonna start making up stories now.
The true one is not too shabby.
ahem
Wait! "Your" what? What were you about to say there?
Nothing. I better get up there and check on–
On your kids' what? Is Raven their mo–
Stop! Just, stop!
Hey, she was just making a stupid joke, okay? It's pretty much what she does.
We don't need more jokes right now. The mood is heavy for a reason.
And since when do you jump to Zoe's defense when she won't shut up? Usually you're the one yelling!
People deal with this stuff differently.

I'm sorry. It's just a few weeks ago I knew where my life was going. I'd finally put all this pirate stuff behind me. I was happy...ish.
And then that-
-My best friend. Someone I love. I mean. Someone who was like a sis-
-that's not even right. I'm so full of it!
I threw myself into the ocean for her, yeah? You guys saw it. Even though she was just kissing-
-grr and why wouldn't she, right? I've pushed her away at every chance.
Believe it or not, I was going to say it. Even if she didn't, I was going to. I mean-
-if there was ever any doubt, she basically took down a whole island for me.
FOR ME!
But what do I do now? I mean, Sunshine is gone but she did her damage and-
-who would have chosen me over her anyway? She was tall and gorgeous and god she was magnetic-
-I'm just...just... pathetic.

What Just happened?
See, that's why you gotta shut up and stop pushing people's buttons.
ME? How is this my fault?
You did it and now you gotta fix it!
I don't know what to do! I'm socially inept. You said so yourself.
Right, and it's your ineptitude that started this, so figure it out.
=huff=
Phew!

Mmmmmm....
good hug.
It's been a tough couple days girls, but this isn't my first rodeo. Remember, I spent most of my life kidnapped by pirates.
I'm going to go up and see Raven and Verity. Thank you guys for listening to all that. Let's keep it between us, okay?
Good talk. You coming?

Ximena!
You got stitches! They look awesome!
What are you doing up?
Verity, look at her, she should be in bed.
I know, but she ordered me to help her out here.
Come on, you stubborn woman. We gotta-
Get off me!

Thank you for saving me. I owe you my life. But you don't run this ship.
Raven, I–
I didn't hear an "Aye, captain!"
Well?
Aye, captain.
Good. Now, you, Quinn and Zoe go muster the rest of the crew. I want everybody up top. I have something to say.
Aye, captain.

Here you are. Here we are. Not all of us, but so many more than anybody off this boat would have guessed, aye?
I look at your beautiful faces and I know what amazing women you are. You're black and blue. Bruised and cut and beaten and drowned. But you've not quit, have you?
No, ma'am.
But we've always been the ones who are beaten and bruised. Women always take punishment. Whether it's fathers or husbands or just men that think they're owed. We all have stitches we don't show off.
But the question is how you react to those stitches. Do you get back up? Do you survive? Do you refuse to let the world get the better of you? Do you?
AYE, CAPTAIN!
And that's what sets you apart. That's what makes you Free Women.

Erg–but not all women survive. Some don't make it out, whether it's a father, a boyfriend, or a stranger. Some women get free the only way they can.
Today, Sunshine is one of those women. Yesterday she walked among us. Today she rests at sea.
Sunshine got free. Someday we'll all join her. Someday we'll all be free for good. Until then, we'll miss her.
TO SUNSHINE ALEXANDER, a free woman!

TO SUNSHINE!

Where the devil?
And where did I get this fly dress?
ahem

Hello here. Who are you?
The queen would like a word with you. Follow me please.
Queen? Which queen is... oh, just one moment.
Okay, sorry, lead on!
This d better be g somewhere mpressive.
Oh yeah, that'll do.
Good, you're awake.

Now I can investigate what my beautiful maids have brought me.

wanted to write a series about Raven – but not just Raven – I wanted her to be surrounded by queer women of every shape, size, and ethnicity that identified as any number of things. In the crew, we have characters who identify as lesbian, bisexual, demisexual, asexual, and even one dealing with questions about their gender. It was important that we represent a wide spectrum of women not just for the sake of representation (thought that is important), but to show that Raven and those around her have built a community for themselves where they're among other queer women who accept their identities as they present them.

And, I guess, it's revolutionary in a way. Raven and her crew have created a safe space in a boat on the middle of the ocean in this wild and untamed world of piracy and magic. And this volume saw that safe space invaded and threatened – as so many real safe spaces have been in the last year. And we see every member of Raven's crew rise up to defend this space, even with their leader out of the game. And that reminds me of something I really wanted to say here.

Thank you. I realize that the proposition of this book is maybe not the most appealing thing from the outside. I am, after all, a straight white cis man writing a whole crew full of diverse queer women. That's a responsibility I take very seriously. I have consulted with a number of women from around the LGBTQ community to make sure that I'm not walking blindly into issues that I'm not aware of. I've listened. I've taken advice. I've changed the text of the book. I don't expect everyone to love it, read it, or even accept it – but I am so grateful to those of you who do. I have spent a little more than eight years writing comics now and I have never had fans who were so eager to spread the word about a book I write as I have with queer women who support this book. You know who you are, but I want to thank Erin, Rachel, Nikki, Juliette, and Tamara specifically. I think the amount of hype you put behind my books may be more than I put out there myself and I am eternally grateful for that.

And on that note, as well as the last pages of this volume, let me say this: I've seen the way that many properties treat their queer female characters and I've been there and watched as you've dealt with that too. You have my word on this: just like Sunshine rises from the water at the end of this volume, I take the responsibility and trust very seriously; this will not be a book where gay and bisexual women will die just because they're gay or bisexual. There are so many more interesting things to do with good characters than kill them. While I can't promise every character will live forever, I promise that if they die, they'll die with agency and heroism and not because of stray bullets and fatalistic romance. You deserve better than that.

-Jeremy

Princess Raven The Pirate Princess

From the Captain's L

There it is, finally, after a year off: the first new volume of Raven. We've been some strange and rough times since last we had a volume of gay pirate-y good the stands and I feel like that makes this one extra special. I wanted to take a mi step back and talk about the experience of making this book.

Raven was created as a result of needing a Princeless Free Comic Book Day story didn't want to regurgitate a story we'd already published and I didn't want to wr anything that was so wrapped up in the continuity of the story that it would be hard t catch up and tell a story in eight pages. So I came up with this idea of Adrienne finding a new princess locked in a tower – someone who wasn't one of her sisters – and reaching out a hand to help. And as it would turn out for Adrienne, the princess in question would be just as capable as she was. It was eight pages and that was supposed to be it.

But it wasn't. I liked Raven too much. It seemed like a good beginning of a story. What if Adrienne met somebody both as capable and as stubborn as her? Adrienne has to prove herself, but Raven has to get revenge. She'll steal Adrienne's dragon to do it, she'll swordfight her on the back of that dragon, but she won't let her drown when she falls into the ocean in her armor. Raven is the rogue to Adrienne's knight. But as it turns out, she was a lot more than that.

Princeless has always been aimed for as wide and young an audience as possible. Beyond that, it is pretty sternly anti-romance as a plot device. I had been asked early on if Adrienne was queer and while I feel pretty comfortable saying that she doesn't really know what she is, I didn't feel comfortable making Adrienne gay. Not because I have any issue with that, but because it's so very beside the point to the plot of that book. Adrienne is proving she doesn't need to be rescued, she doesn't need a man, that she is capable of rescuing herself. It's not about rejecting men because she has a romantic interest in women. It's about rejecting men because she doesn't need them. Those two things aren't necessarily mutually exclusive, but I thought it had the potential to muddy the thematic waters of that book.

But I knew from even those first few pages that Raven was gay. Once we fleshed out book 3 of Princeless (where Raven is introduced), I felt like it was pretty firmly established. She never exactly says it, but she flirts with Adrienne pretty hard. To me, it's in a way charming that Raven flirts so hard out of the gate and that Adrienne continues to be clueless. And I saw a lot of LGBTQ readers reading the book and posting about Raven's facial expressions and ultimately forsaking the relationship (and just how hard they related). I also saw a lot of straight readers that seemed to have no idea that any of that had happened. I had wanted to write more Raven as I wrote those issues of Princeless, but that relationship with the readership was what really galvanized it.

Page 6 Progression

Page 6:

Panel 1: Quinn puts her arm out in front, inviting Zoe to lead.

QUINN
By all means, this is your skill set.

ZOE
What is?

QUINN
Snooping, prying, finding people.

ZOE
I…

Panel 2: Zoe strides out in front of Quinn, dramatically proud.

ZOE
You know what, I choose to take that as a compliment.

QUINN
Hey, you are forever bothering me. I notice these things.

Panel 3: Zoe is walking backwards again, this time closer to Quinn.

ZOE
Hey, to be fair, I mostly bother you with things I know you're into.

QUINN
And what am I into?

ZOE
Punching, kicking, competing, making fun of thing wi—

Panel 4: Quinn grabs Zoe and pulls her to her suddenly.

QUINN
Zo!

Page 6 Inks

Page 6 Thumbnail

Page 6 Progression

Page 6 Colors

Page 19 Progression

Page 19:

Panel 1: Raven stands above the rest of the crew near the wheel. She is still supported largely by Verity, but has managed to straighten herself up a bit.

RAVEN
Here you are. Here we are. Not all of us, but so many more than anybody off this boat would have guessed, aye?

Panel 2: The crew stands entranced, listening to and watching Raven.

RAVEN (OFF PANEL)
I look at your beautiful faces and I know what amazing women you are. You're black and blue. Bruised and cut and beaten and drowned. But you've not quit, have you?

CREW (TOGETHER)
No, ma'am.

Panel 3: Raven tries to step forward, putting her good hand on the railing. Verity assists gently.

RAVEN
But we've always been the ones who are beaten and bruised. Women always take punishment. Whether it's fathers or husbands or just men that think they're owed. We all have stitches we don't show off.

Panel 4: Raven pushes up on the railing.

RAVEN
But the question is how you react to those stitches. Do you get back up? Do you survive? Do you refuse to let the world get the better of you? Do you?

CREW
AYE, CAPTAIN

Panel 5: Raven smiles.

RAVEN
And that's what sets you apart.
That's what makes you Free Women.

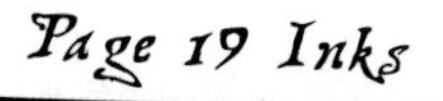

Page 19 Thumbnail

Page 19 Progression

Page 19 Colors